The New Teacher

The New Teacher

Dominique Demers

Translated by Sander Berg

Illustrations by Tony Ross

ALMA JUNIOR

ALMA BOOKS LTD
3 Castle Yard
Richmond
Surrey TW10 6TF
United Kingdom
www.almabooks.com

The New Teacher first published in French by Éditions Québec Amérique
in 1994
This translation first published by Alma Books Ltd in 2016
© Dominique Demers, 1994

Translation © Sander Berg, 2016

Dominique Demers and Sander Berg assert their moral right to be
identified as the author and translator respectively of this work in
accordance with the Copyright, Designs and Patents Act 1988

Inside and cover illustrations by Tony Ross. Illustrations first
published in France by Éditions Gallimard Jeunesse
© Éditions Gallimard Jeunesse, Paris, 2003

Printed in Great Britain by CPI Group (UK) Ltd, Croydon CR0 4YY

ISBN: 978-1-84688-399-6

Contents

The New Teacher

Chapter 1

She's Completely Bonkers!

Normally teachers walk very fast. They're always in a hurry. Their heels go click! clack! click! clack! click! in the corridor. That morning, it was different. Our new teacher seemed to take her time. We heard two or three little tap-taps. Then, nothing. As if our new teacher were dawdling in the corridor instead of hurrying up.

The class was silent. You could have heard a pea roll across the floor. We were all dying with curiosity to see what our new teacher looked like. We'd been talking about nothing else all week. No one knew what this mysterious person from another town might look like. Our old teacher was having a baby. She'd left us to look after her big round tummy.

Suddenly the door opened and a very tall and very thin lady appeared. She was wearing a strange hat. It was like a witch's hat, except that the top was round instead of long and pointy. Her dress, however, was nothing like a witch's outfit. It was an old-fashioned evening gown with bows and lace, a bit faded but still pretty.

And that was not all. Our new teacher didn't wear tiny shoes with high heels like the others. She was wearing big leather ones with thick soles. These were shoes made for hiking in forests, climbing up mountains or walking to the ends of the earth... Not for going to school at any rate.

We all opened our eyes as wide as planets, and quite a few jaws dropped too. As always, it was Alex who spoke first.

"She's not a teacher: she's a scarecrow!"

Some of us chuckled. Then, nothing. Our eyes were riveted on that weird old lady. She slowly walked to the window, the one from where you can see the little wood where Matthieu and Julie meet to kiss. Our new teacher looked out of the window. Then she smiled. She had a lovely smile.

Normally teachers present themselves. They say: "Good morning children, I am Mrs Lagalipette." Or else: "Hello, my name is Nathalie." Their voice is soft or shrill, their tone harsh or cheerful. You get an idea who you're dealing with. But our new teacher didn't say a word.

She went to her desk, and then I realized she didn't even have a bag with books or anything. That funny old teacher had come to school empty-handed! If we forget our school bag, we have to go and see the head teacher, Mr Cracpote, and explain why. I always find that a little difficult, because if you forget something, you forget something. That's all there is to it. You can't really explain why.

Then at last our beanpole of a teacher sat down. Everyone was holding their breath. We'd finally find out if she was obsessed with maths or with spelling tests. Or if she was the kind who makes a fuss about nothing.

There are teachers who go berserk when words go any which way on the page instead of neatly staying on the lines of our exercise books. Others panic at the slightest noise. A mouse's fart would wake them up at night.

What I wanted to find out most of all was if our new teacher liked – a little, a lot or an awful lot – to put people in detention. Because with the old one, let's just say I got my fair share.

Our new teacher was now well and truly installed behind her desk, but she didn't seem to be in a hurry. She quietly smoothed out the hem of her dress and then, without even looking at us, she delicately took off her huge hat, holding it by its broad brim, and placed it on the desk.

Her grey hair was held together in a bun. She wore her hair like many old ladies do, except that she had a strange object on her head. It was the size of, say, a tangerine, a golf ball or a big marble. A few pupils got up to have a better look, and Benoît even climbed onto his desk.

It was a pebble!

Very carefully, our new teacher picked it up, as if it were a very rare and fragile

object. Then – believe it or not – she gave it a huge smile, gently stroking it with the tip of her index finger, like a parent tickling a child!

Then she finally spoke. But not to us. To her pebble!

"Hello my pumpkin. Aww, poor little peanut. I woke you up, didn't I? I'm sorry. I was feeling a bit lonely... We're in the new class now. Are they friendly? I don't know yet. They're all looking at me as if I've forgotten to put my dress on. As if I'm walking around in my pyjamas or in my knickers. I'm going to have to say hello to them. But first I wanted to have a chat with you. Don't worry... I'm feeling better already."

The teacher put her pebble on the corner of her desk and, for a few seconds, I had the impression it was alive, that it would start to yap, grunt or miaow. From the back of the class Alex shouted, with his usual tact:

"She's bonkers!"

I looked at my friend Léa. She tapped her forehead with her index finger a couple of times. I knew exactly what she meant. And I agreed. Our new teacher was stark raving mad. Off her rocker. Barmy. Mental.

The class began to be noisy. Everyone was wondering what to do in a situation like this. Warn Miss Lamerlotte in the classroom next door? Get Mr Cracpote? Or the police, a doctor, the fire brigade?

Suddenly our new teacher got up. She slowly walked around her desk, and when she got to the front she sat down… on top of her desk.

Even sitting down our new teacher was tall.
She cleared her throat and gave us a smile.
Immediately the class fell silent. Everyone
stopped whispering, as if spellbound.

"Hello…"

Her voice was reedy but cheerful, with a hint
of shyness.

"Would you like to do some… err… maths?"
she asked.

No one answered. We were all a bit shocked.
Then she addressed Guillaume.

"You, would you like to start the day with
some divisions or a bit of geometry?"

Guillaume can't stand anything that even remotely resembles a number. Although our new teacher had made quite an impression on him, he still managed to reply:

"No... No, ma'am... Err... No, miss. Err... Not at all."

The funniest thing was that our new teacher seemed to be over the moon with his reply.

"Would you like to do a spelling test then?"

This time Alex didn't hesitate. He replied:

"No. We all hate spelling tests here. They get on our nerves..."

The way he said it almost sounded like a threat. Alex enjoys being the class clown, and our new teacher gave him a delighted smile. Her eyes sparkled with joy.

"Really? That's great! Me too."

That's literally what our new teacher said. And she sounded perfectly sincere. That's when it occurred to me that perhaps this weird old lady is from another planet. That normally she's small and green with three eyes in her head. Her pebble must be some sort of two-way radio allowing her to stay in touch with a marvellous spaceship twirling around in space, billions of light years away from our classroom.

The worst thing was that, basically, I probably wasn't far wrong.

Chapter 2

Dear Toothbrush

After a week, we still didn't know all that much about our new teacher. Her name was Miss Charlotte, and she came from a faraway village in the north of Quebec. At least, that's what she told us. Alex swore she made it all up. He was convinced she was a spy. Those sweet nothings she addressed to her pebble were some kind of secret code. She may disguise herself as an eccentric old lady, but she was actually a formidable woman who had slit other people's throats and had endured the most awful forms of torture.

Miss Charlotte often talked to her pebble, and always out loud. She called it "my precious darling" or "my own little Gertrude", or "my beautiful sweet cupcake". I found it hard to imagine that these messages were being decoded by spies. Anyway, however strange it may sound, after a few days we almost got used to her pebble.

What we did in class with Miss Charlotte was nothing like what normally goes on in schools. And as far as schools are concerned, let's just say I know my onions. My dad and I have moved house loads and I've been to tons of schools!

Every morning Miss Charlotte would ask us about our projects. The first time, no one answered. We were too baffled. Miss Charlotte walked through the classroom with her eyes wide open in amazement. Looking gutted, she just muttered:

"Well… OK then. If you wish. This morning we'll be bored."

She was sitting right there, in front of us and on top of her desk, heaving heart-rending sighs. After a couple of very, very long minutes, Marie put up her hand and asked if we could talk among ourselves. That was a brilliant idea. Ever since the first bell I'd been counting down the minutes until morning break, because I was dying to tell Léa that Tartiflette, my cat, had had kittens that night.

Miss Charlotte gave us permission, and we chatted until break. When we got back, Simon suggested we play a game of football. The weather was beautiful, and even though I'm not mad about ball games, I was delighted that Miss Charlotte said yes. The idea that we could run around in the playground when our old teachers would normally make us do times tables made any sport sound interesting.

We formed two teams, but our side was one player short. Without saying a word, Miss Charlotte hitched up her dress, taking the hem up to her waist and retying her belt to keep it all in place.

At the start, Miss Charlotte was as clumsy as can be. You'd think she'd never seen a football in her life. Let alone a goal! But after half-time she passed the ball brilliantly to Alex, who scored a goal. A stroke of luck? Not at all! Immediately afterwards, our new teacher kicked the ball straight into the back of the net. And three goals later we all realized that big old Charlotte had a terrific shot.

At 5–4 the game was tight. Shouts were ringing out from all sides. I was dripping with sweat, as were the others. Miss Charlotte's bun

was a mess, and her dress had become undone. We were too busy to notice Mr Cracpote. Mélanie nearly suffocated when she charged into his big, soft belly. I heard a cry. Everyone stopped.

Mr Cracpote was furious. He looked for our new teacher. When he spotted her, her hair a riot and the hem of her dress dangling down bizarrely, his eyes widened.

"Good day Mr Laporte! Would you care to join us?" Miss Charlotte asked him, beaming with joy.

After a huge effort, Mr Cracpote managed to force a smile. It was plain to see he didn't know how to react.

"Oh, please! Come and join us, Mr... Laporte!" Alex begged.

It was the best way to save Miss Charlotte. Acting as if it were perfectly natural and invite Mr Cracpote to join in.

The plan worked. Mr Cracpote muttered something and then he left. I think he would have preferred to clean all the toilets in the school with a toothbrush rather than play a match with us.

On the second day, Miss Charlotte suggested a new timetable. The first hours of the day would be set aside for "compulsory stuff": French, maths and English. Our new teacher was quite good at explaining things, and Alex stopped mucking about, because we were all keen to get to the "fun stuff".

Miss Charlotte had reckoned that if we worked hard and did a little bit of homework every evening we could get through the "compulsory stuff" in two hours, which left us exactly three hours and fifty-eight minutes for "fun stuff". After a few days, we had a whole raft of ideas on how to fill all that extra free time.

Guillaume did a magic show. Miss Charlotte got scared when he proposed to saw her in half and put her back together again, but he was just kidding.

Judith, who's a bit stuck-up and dreams of becoming a TV presenter, made us taste five kinds of chocolate-chip cookies blindfolded, like they do in the ads.

Martin stole the show, though, with his grasshoppers. Everyone wanted to eat one, but there were only seven of them. Mélanie thought they tasted like soft peanut butter, and Éric like a pizza margherita. Léa said their little legs tickle your throat when you swallow them.

Manon came up with a brilliant game: setting records. Everyone has to pick something he or she is good at and then challenge the rest of the class. Yesterday Éric ate eleven biscuits in fifty-four seconds without drinking a drop of water. The day before Geneviève held her breath for one hundred and nine seconds. Simon put his leg around his neck – like a real contortionist! – and Aude blew a bubble with her gum the size of a grapefruit, ending up with her eyelashes stuck together and all.

We all wanted to know what Miss Charlotte's speciality was. She was sure to have some extraordinary gift or mysterious powers, but no one dared to ask her. Last Thursday I couldn't resist any more, and I asked. There was a very long silence. Then Miss Charlotte simply began to talk.

It was even more wonderful than anything we could have imagined. I'd have never believed that mere words could be so powerful.

First she told us a horror story. For a few minutes the classroom disappeared. We were transported to a dark cemetery crawling with zombies. It was a stormy night, as cold as ice. The frosted branches rattled like the bones of a skeleton. A sickening smell filled the air. Ghosts were spying on us from the shadows. All of a sudden a hideous creature leapt towards us, landing a few metres away. A voice cried out. A werewolf was devouring us with its famished eyes, its terrible fangs glistening in the deep, dark night.

No sooner had we finished the first story – the shivers still running down our spines – than Miss Charlotte took us to a dazzling desert in the East. I felt the flanks of my camel heave beneath my feet while the animal sped towards the horizon, its large hooves pounding the sand and throwing up jets of dust, which were quickly swept away by the howling wind. Long after Miss Charlotte had stopped talking, I could still feel the grains of sand between my fingers.

Every day from that afternoon on, Miss Charlotte made us laugh, cry, weep and travel to faraway places with her stories, wherever she got them from. When she took us to the high seas to hear singing whales up close, I told myself that I too would love to paint pictures of waves in people's minds with nothing but words. And the morning when pirates attacked our ship, Alex told me he'd felt the cold steel of a cutlass against his cheek.

Friday afternoon that first week, Emma was late for school. Miss Charlotte was talking to her pebble while we were finishing off some sums. Emma sat down at her desk without greeting anyone. A few minutes later she burst into tears.

There are various ways of crying. The way Emma cried made it clear she was frightfully upset. Zoé, her best friend, wanted to comfort her and find out what the matter was. But Emma refused to speak.

We all thought Miss Charlotte would get involved. Our old teacher would have gently taken Emma to one side and forced her to tell everything. But Miss Charlotte calmly put her stone under her hat, sat down on her desk and asked for our attention.

This time our new teacher didn't invent a story. She told us a little bit about herself. A long time ago – and given that Miss Charlotte is quite old, this could be five or fifty years ago – a long time ago, then, something awful had happened to her. Something really terrible. So terrible that she no longer felt like eating, running or sleeping. I think Miss Charlotte had even lost the will to live.

The worst thing was that she was alone. Without parents, neighbours or friends. She had no one to talk to, no one to comfort her. Then, one day, she picked up a pebble. She called it Gertrude and started talking to it.

Miss Charlotte said that we can invent anything. That in our heads there are millions of countries, characters and planets. It's up to us to bring them to life. And you shouldn't worry about what other people might think.

"Everyone has the right to talk to their pencil sharpener or their trainers. They don't replace our actual friends, but sometimes it's just great to create characters and share our secrets with them."

Miss Charlotte is really quite convincing. When she speaks, her eyes light up and sparkle. We are all a little spellbound by her. I don't know if she's aware of her powers, but the next morning Léo was talking to his toothbrush in the corridor, and Mélanie to a fork.

During lunch break, Mr Cracpote found Guillaume deep in conversation with his pencil case.

"Who are you talking to?" our head teacher wanted to know.

"To my granddad," Guillaume replied calmly.

That's when I realized that the arrival of Miss Charlotte was really going to change our lives.

Chapter 3

You Crispy Duck, You!

Miss Charlotte's lessons had become suspicious. At any time of the day we could see Mr Cracpote's fat nose pressed against the tiny window of our classroom door.

The head teacher was spying on us when Charles-Antoine, the class boffin, gave a one-hour presentation on his ants. No one knew Charles-Antoine bred ant colonies at home. He brought a fish tank filled with sand and explained how ants communicate by stroking the tips of each other's antennae and how they dig their subterranean galleries and tunnels. They even make rooms with doors for their cocooned babies. It was fascinating!

Normally Charles-Antoine isn't very talkative. During break he often sits alone in a corner and reads. Alex says Charles-Antoine thinks he's too clever to hang out with us. I just think Charles-Antoine is different. And when he talks about winged queen ants courageously breaking off their beautiful wings in order to squeeze themselves into a tiny hole to lay eggs, Charles-Antoine is very handsome. You'd almost say he shines from within.

Mr Cracpote must have felt reassured on the day of the ants. Charles-Antoine had written loads of information on the board and he spoke at length, like a proper teacher. All the pupils listened to him quietly, without moving or talking. But on the day of the spaghetti, our head teacher got very worried again.

Miss Charlotte had given us a problem beforehand. How many strings of spaghetti do you need to go all the way round the classroom? She didn't want us to find out the dimensions of the room and then divide them by the length of a strand of spaghetti. No, no. She wanted us to just guess or imagine it.

I made a quick calculation. I reckoned a string of spaghetti is about eight inches long, that's about twenty centimetres. Easy peasy! As for the walls, that was harder. I tried to imagine the length of a metre in my head and to figure out how many I'd need to get from one end of the wall to the other. Twenty-three, give or take. Multiplied by four walls, that was ninety-two. Dividing the length of the wall by the strands of spaghetti, after converting metres to centimetres, I finally concluded that you'd need three hundred and seven strands of spaghetti to go all around the classroom.

Miss Charlotte wrote down each pupil's response, after which we forgot all about the "spaghetti problem". A few days later our teacher came to school with a yellow-and-red wheelbarrow. Imagine the faces of the pupils and the teachers in the playground when she made her way towards the main

entrance. People still hadn't got over Miss Charlotte's outfit – she continued to wear the same old dress and her incredible hat – and there she was, adding a wheelbarrow to her eccentricities.

That remarkable vehicle contained two bulging green bags. It wasn't until we were inside with the door shut firmly behind us that we discovered what was in them. They were filled with… spaghetti. Thousands of strands of soft spaghetti, still lukewarm and cooked al dente.

"Cooked pasta sticks to walls," explained Miss Charlotte, with an enigmatic smile on her lips.

We rolled up our sleeves and started to stick the spaghetti to the walls. Meanwhile Miss Charlotte wrote the names of every pupil on the board, followed by their solutions to the spaghetti problem from the other day.

Our teacher had cooked way too much spaghetti. We could have really stuffed ourselves! Even without sauce it was yummy.

Afterwards, we had to count all the strands of spaghetti stuck to the walls again and again, because each time we arrived at a different total. After the third counting Guillaume announced there were three hundred and seventy-seven of them. And Éric yelled: "YABBA DABBA DOO!" like Fred Flintstone always does, because he nearly got it right.

That's when I saw Mr Cracpote's fat nose pressed against the window of our classroom door.

Miss Charlotte caught my eye, after which she looked at the door and back at me again. A mysterious smile still played on her lips. It seemed our new teacher didn't give a hoot about what the head teacher might think. For a few seconds I thought that Mr Cracpote would blow a fuse, fling open the door and sack Miss Charlotte on the spot. He was visibly angry, but he didn't do anything, and after a few seconds he slunk off.

Things got really bad three weeks to the day after the arrival of our new teacher. That

Monday afternoon, Matthieu called Vu Tran a sticky pork belly...

It wasn't the first time Matthieu had used foreign fare to wind Vu up. Their fights always start with a single dish, but after a couple of minutes Matthieu usually throws the whole menu at him:

"You crispy duck, you! Prawn dumpling! Mouldy old spring roll!

And Vu, who has perhaps never even tasted crispy duck, flies into a rage. And at each insult, instead of calling Matthieu an old custard pie, a fat sausage or a piece of runny cheese, he thumps him. The two of them are always at each other's throats, because Matthieu is the official boyfriend of Julie, who has taken quite a shine to Vu and often makes eyes at him.

After the insults and the first blow, it's always a little tense. We stop playing to see which of the two will get the worst of it.

That day it was Vu. When the bell rang, he had a bloody nose and scratches on his right cheek, where Matthieu had dug his nails

into him. Vu was dabbing his nose with some toilet paper and Matthieu was gingerly feeling his eye, which was beginning to turn black, when Miss Charlotte entered the classroom twittering away to her pebble.

"What a lovely day it is outside, isn't it, my beautiful Gertrude? You can really smell the spring in the air. How about going for a little walk later this evening, at least if..."

Our new teacher stopped talking when she saw Vu. She opened her eyes wide and her face turned white. She stifled a cry with her hand, and then she rushed towards Vu as if he'd fallen down the twenty-second storey of a building.

"What's going on? How are you feeling? Is anyone else hurt?"

To be honest, I nearly burst out laughing. It was so funny. Our new teacher really *was* odd. Matthieu and Vu had a fight, which is hardly the end of the world. But on hearing Miss Charlotte you'd think the Third World War had just broken out. She seemed ready to declare a state of emergency and alert the doctors, the ambulance drivers, the police and the fire brigade…

"It was that clown who hit me," said Vu, looking at Matthieu, his dark eyes throwing daggers.

Miss Charlotte turned to the accused, whose eye was swollen and rimmed with purple.

We all heard the little dull thud of Gertrude falling onto the floor. Miss Charlotte was so stunned, so sad and horrified, that she'd dropped her precious pebble.

Charles-Antoine ran towards Gertrude to pick her up and, a little embarrassed, handed her over to Miss Charlotte. Our new teacher took her pebble and put it in one of the pockets of her large dress. She sat down on her desk and gave each and every one of us a long, hard and strangely serious look.

The minutes went by in slow motion and in utter silence. Miss Charlotte seemed to be thinking very deeply. Suddenly she asked:

"These fights, do they happen a lot?"

A lot… What does that mean, "a lot"? Every day? Every week? Every break? Off the top of my head, I'd say two or three times a week. No more, I reckon.

That's exactly what Chloé said. But judging from the look on Miss Charlotte's face, we all understood that for her that was far too often.

A stunned silence reigned in the classroom. Miss Charlotte appeared to be so appalled that Matthieu blurted out, as a kind of excuse:

"I just got a bit carried away, that's all. Normally we don't hurt each other this badly…"

The poor lad didn't know what to say next. And, really, he should have kept his mouth shut, because what he went on to say unleashed a storm.

"And besides, we're not the only ones. Yesterday Alex pushed Éric into the wall. And last week—"

Miss Charlotte interrupted him. She'd understood that all of us got into a fight every now and again. And it was all too clear that our new teacher came from some bizarre country or faraway planet where punch-ups are unheard of.

"I don't want to hear another word!" she said categorically.

Then Miss Charlotte got up, slowly smoothed out the creases in her dress and readjusted her hat. She walked to the door with measured steps and a straight back. Before disappearing she simply turned round and told us:

"You can tell Mr Laporte that I hand in my notice. He'll receive my official resignation by post."

And she left us.

Chapter 4

A Letter and Seven Garden Gnomes

"What a disaster!"

Alex repeated these words time and again. The other pupils kept their pain and fear to themselves.

In a few seconds we'd come to realize just how important Miss Charlotte was in our lives. What upset us wasn't just the idea of having to spend all day long doing maths and grammar again with some other teacher. No. It was the idea of never seeing Miss Charlotte again with her smile, her mad hat and her pebble. Of no longer being swept away by her stories or coming up with cool projects... But worst of all was the terrible thought of losing Miss Charlotte.

"She's just having a tantrum! My little brother does it all the time. She'll come back," said Fred with a voice that sounded anything but confident.

But we all knew he didn't really believe what he said. Miss Charlotte had left us because she couldn't stand the fact that we hit each other and call each other all sorts of names. Maybe where she was from people simply never do that. One thing was certain: Miss Charlotte was allergic to violence.

Someone knocked on our classroom door. A head peeked through the half-open door. A few pupils let out a cry.

Mr Cracpote!

"Is Miss Charlotte not with you?"

His tone was vaguely threatening. We realized immediately that our head teacher must never find out what really happened.

I took a deep breath.

"She went to the toilet, sir. To the *ladies'* toilet."

CHAPTER 4

My tone was vaguely threatening too. Surely Mr Cracpote wouldn't dare to go *there* to check on her.

To make it sound more believable, I added: "If you want, I can go and find her…"

Our head teacher didn't insist and left. Phew!

We had to act quickly. Come up with an idea, think up a plan to make Miss Charlotte come back.

First of all we decided that Miss Charlotte's departure had to remain a secret. No one must find out. Children can't just run away from school, and we guessed the same goes for teachers.

Everyone had different ideas, but they were all too elaborate and complicated. Finally we decided to write to Miss Charlotte. It was a very straightforward solution, a poor little doubtful plan, but we all put our hearts into it.

We knew that Miss Charlotte lived in an old house at the edge of town that had long stood empty. Once we'd written the letter, everyone wanted to deliver it to Miss Charlotte. Fortunately Alex pointed out that a delegation of thirty pupils carrying out a supposedly secret mission was not a very clever idea.

We had a vote. We only had to choose a class representative, but to us it was as important as electing the prime minister of a country. Charles-Antoine, my ant king, was chosen to represent us. I was happy for him.

But the icing on the cake was that he invited me to come with him.

"It will be less suspicious if there are two of us," he said.

I tried not to show just how pleased I was, but when I said "S-s-sure", I felt myself go weak in the knees. I had just discovered that Charles-Antoine has the most gorgeous green eyes, even more beautiful than my cat Tartiflette's.

When we set out we felt a bit self-conscious. But then I told Charles-Antoine his ants had made a huge impression on me, and he promised to invite me over to his house to see them. After that, the two of us chatted until we reached the street where Miss Charlotte lived.

The house was not as run-down as I had imagined. There were pretty curtains with flowers behind the windows and… the Seven Dwarfs as garden gnomes on the steps leading to her front door.

I laughed.

That was so typical of Miss Charlotte.

Charles-Antoine knocked on the door. We waited for a long time. Then he knocked again. Three times. In my head I counted to fifty. Nothing.

That's when I felt the urge to cry, just like that, standing next to Charles-Antoine in front of Miss Charlotte's door with those Seven Dwarfs staring at me.

Our teacher had really left us.

"Come on! Let's look through the windows," Charles-Antoine suggested.

Through the curtains we could see the kitchen table. And on it there was… a large hat. Like a witch's hat, but with a round top instead of a long and pointy one.

Miss Charlotte was still living there! She hadn't left town yet.

There was no letter box. So we put our letter between Dopey's hands. There it was in plain sight and didn't risk being carried off by the wind.

Coming back from who knows where, Miss Charlotte would be able to read what we had written.

Dear Miss Charlotte,
The whole class is sad. We miss your stories, we miss Gertrude, we miss your spaghetti. We miss you, Miss Charlotte.

We didn't know you were allergic to fights. How could we?

You are different, Miss Charlotte. But we like you like that. It's why we love you. So if you come back, we won't fight any more. Promise. It won't be easy, but that's just tough luck.

Come back, Miss Charlotte. Please!

The whole class had signed the letter, and our names were scribbled all over the page.

Chapter 5

Such a Rude Gorilla!

The next morning the class was quiet. We waited, our hearts pounding. Would Miss Charlotte return?

When we heard her funny tap-taps in the corridor there was a thunderous applause. We were so chuffed!

Our new teacher entered and walked calmly over to the window to daydream a bit, like she'd done on the first day. Then she sat down, gently took off her hat and tickled Gertrude a bit. Life had returned to normality. We were happy.

That morning we did three pages of French and four maths problems in under two hours.

Everyone worked really hard. After that, Miss Charlotte told us a story.

Two children, Benjamin and Camille, are kidnapped by bandits as they come out of school. After a few days of being driven around in the back of a lorry, they manage to escape and discover – how can it be? – that they are in the middle of the jungle. The air is heavy and the heat unbearable. The place is teeming with huge plants. Lianas come tumbling down from above and amazing birds are letting out shrill cries.

Suddenly the children hear a rustling sound. Someone or something is coming their way with great stealth. The steps come closer. Horrified, Benjamin and Camille see a dark shape making its way slowly through the undergrowth. It makes a sound somewhere between a grunt and a growl. A panther!

The children already see themselves reduced to minced meat in the belly of the big cat, when a gigantic hairy animal lifts them off the ground.

Rubbery plants fly by. Benjamin and Camille may have escaped the claws of a panther, but what's this huge creature clutching them in its paws? The animal's heartbeat is pounding in their ears. It's so loud! What's more, this large beast stinks and its rough hairs scratch their cheeks. But, strangely, the children feel almost safe.

Suddenly Benjamin cried out:

"A gorilla!"

The penny had dropped…

Miss Charlotte stopped right there, promising to continue with the story the next day. We couldn't wait!

The most amazing thing was not so much what happened to the characters, but what happened to *us*. We hadn't just heard her story. We'd been in it. For real.

I could have described in minute detail the back of the lorry where the two heroes were held captive. There was a rusty chain in the corner, and next to it an opened tin of ravioli with a mouldy bit of sauce stuck to the bottom.

I'd noticed how the running gorilla crushed a large insect with a purple shell. I even remember the noise it made – scrrroinch! – and the foul yellow liquid that squirted from its body.

Where did the tin of ravioli come from? And the squashed insect? Miss Charlotte hadn't mentioned these details when she told the story. And I wasn't the only one who had seen, felt or heard strange things.

Louis swore a magnificent bird, with wings as large as sails on a ship and feathers a hundred times more brightly coloured than those of a common parrot, had landed on his shoulder. Magali had stumbled upon two hissing snakes between her feet. And poor Emma was retching after the gorilla had belched straight into her face.

Every morning from that day on, Miss Charlotte invented a new episode of the jungle adventure. The rest of the day everyone worked on their projects.

And Mr Cracpote became more and more nervous and anxious.

He was worried sick, tore his hair out and bit his nails. Our head teacher was no longer content to press his fat nose against the glass pane in the door for a few seconds. He entered without knocking, at any old time.

One afternoon he opened the door when Fred – who is a bit of a boffin when it comes to everything mechanical, electronic, robotic or anything else that ticks – had just taken apart the classroom clock. Mr Cracpote's face went crimson. With her soft voice Miss Charlotte reassured our head teacher that in an hour or two the clock would be on the wall again and its hands move like before.

Another time he came in when Matthieu and Julie were... kissing each other! Miss Charlotte quickly explained that the two lovebirds were playing a scene from *Romeo and Juliet* by Mr Shakespeare, which was true. Matthieu and Julie had even learnt their lines off by heart. But Mr Cracpote announced indignantly that nine-year-old children should not be kissing each other.

"Under no circumstances. Theatre or no theatre," he added furiously.

A few days later miss Lamerlotte, who teaches next door, slammed the door in disgust. She'd come to borrow some chalk, but what she saw quickly made her forget why she'd come. Clémence was cleaning Miss Charlotte's desk, which was covered in a puddle of green, smoking, foul-smelling froth that vaguely reeked of rotting eggs. Poor Clémence! Her scientific experiment had failed.

Tension in school was mounting day by day. Pupils from other classes were asking us no end of questions about Miss Charlotte, and a number of parents had rung the head master to ask for more information about the one they called "the alien".

Maybe we should have stopped thinking up new projects for a while. But it was so exciting... And also, it was as if Miss Charlotte transmitted her energy to us. We all felt a bit more confident about ourselves. That's what happens when you have a teacher who strolls through the corridor twittering to herself, with a huge hat on her head and a pebble in the hollow of her hand, without ever worrying about what other people might say or think.

Miss Charlotte had been teaching in our school for a month when, one Thursday afternoon, Mathilde Buisson's mother came to fetch her daughter on the stroke of two to take her to the dentist.

The snag is that Mrs Buisson opened the door just when Thomas's trained rat pulled off a stunt on the flying trapeze for the fourth time.

Thomas had been training his rat for weeks. He'd read various books on how to train animals and had built a flying trapeze, like the ones you see in the circus, but smaller and made from clothes hangers.

It seems Mrs Buisson can't tell a rat from a dinosaur. She screamed so loudly when she

saw Jojo (that's Thomas's rat's name) that Mr Cracpote and a string of other teachers immediately came rushing to our classroom. Mr Cracpote didn't want to listen to Miss Charlotte's explanations and sent Thomas and Jojo home.

The next day, Benoît gave a presentation on life in the Middle Ages. He'd done masses of research. Unfortunately, Mr Cracpote had chosen the worst moment to spy on us again. Benoît explained how people of that period used to eat with their hands. To liven up his presentation he'd brought a shepherd's pie and began to stuff himself in front of us, using neither knife nor fork. His hands, arms, cheeks, nose and even eyebrows were covered in mashed potato, with bits of corn and minced meat everywhere.

This time Mr Cracpote didn't say anything. He simply shut the door behind him. But the way our head teacher acted didn't bode well, and I felt a shiver run down my spine.

For a few days we didn't have any trouble. The next Monday I'd forgotten my dad's alarm clock in my desk. Alex had used it for one of his projects. The sound that thing makes is enough to wake a sleeping diplodocus. So I thought I'd better get it back as soon as possible.

It was only a quarter to five and the teachers' cars were still parked outside the school. And yet the corridors were surprisingly deserted and quiet. Then I heard voices coming from

Miss Lamerlotte's classroom as I walked past. And through the little window in the door I saw all the teachers gathered around Mr Cracpote. All the teachers apart from one: Miss Charlotte.

I put my ear to the door to eavesdrop on their conversation. After a few minutes I nearly let out a cry. My legs started to shake.

I felt like making a dash for it, but I managed to get a grip on myself. I had to. I walked away slowly, without making the floorboards creak. But as soon as I'd reached the main entrance and shut the door, I ran as if all the panthers of the jungle were at my heels.

I rushed straight to Charles-Antoine's house.

Chapter 6

Our Teacher Is a Fake!

I told Charles-Antoine everything.

Mr Cracpote had discovered that Miss Charlotte wasn't a real teacher. She didn't have any qualifications! She claimed to have worked in various schools that didn't even exist. The head teacher was going to invite all the parents to a meeting the next evening. He wanted to sack Miss Charlotte.

While I was talking, I had been twisting Charles-Antoine's bedspread. I was a little embarrassed when I saw the crumpled cloth around me. But Charles-Antoine smiled and took my hand in his. That felt good.

"We have to warn all the pupils!" he decided.

Charles-Antoine seemed sure of himself and very determined. He added with a firm voice:

"We're going to save Miss Charlotte!"

That's when I had an idea. I can't remember how I thought of it, and I wasn't sure if my plan would work, but never mind. We had to try something.

Once more Charles-Antoine heard me out without saying a word. He clapped his hands in approval and then he said:

"To work!"

We had a lot on our plate.

Chapter 7

A Dramatic Turn of Events

The next day all the pupils in the school received a letter for their parents: special meeting at 7 p.m. in the assembly hall. Things were going just as we'd hoped.

The pupils from Miss Charlotte's class had already received another letter as soon as they'd arrived: a secret letter written by Charles-Antoine and me, addressing only them and not their parents.

Everything went according to plan.

During lunch break our class met in the little wood where Matthieu and Julie meet to kiss. I explained my idea, and together we created an action plan.

We agreed to meet again at 6 p.m. It was vital that our parents didn't see us!

At around twenty to seven, Mr Cracpote went into the assembly hall with some of the teachers. Not long afterwards, the first parents arrived. At 7 p.m. the assembly hall was full.

Mr Cracpote repeated what he'd said the previous evening in Miss Lamerlotte's classroom. Some parents loudly expressed their indignation.

"But that's unacceptable!"

"That woman could be dangerous!"

"Something has to be done at once…"

"And more than just giving her the sack… We ought to sue her!"

Then Charles-Antoine gave the signal. The heavy red curtains opened up and the assembled parents saw Miss Charlotte's whole class on stage, in front of them.

The pupils were waiting silently for their new teacher to arrive.

That was my plan. Instead of explaining to the parents that Miss Charlotte wasn't

dangerous and that we were very fond of her
and that we'd learnt a million things with her,
I thought we could show it to them. Just like
at the theatre.

And I was to play the role of Miss Charlotte!
I'd spent a good deal of the night turning the
witch's hat of my old Halloween costume
into Miss Charlotte's hat. Charles-Antoine
had lent me one of his granny's dresses and a
pair of hiking boots.

Now it was my turn. I had to go on stage
and pretend to be Miss Charlotte. But then,
in the wings, I panicked. I had a terrible stage
fright! I nearly skedaddled.

Miss Charlotte's future depended on me. I
only had a few minutes to charm the parents.
And, above all, to convince them not to sack
our new teacher.

The audience was waiting, but I was planted
to the spot, incapable of moving an inch. My
feet seemed to have taken root. Then, to pluck
up my courage, I lifted up my hat and took the
little pebble from the top of my head.

It wasn't Gertrude. It was just an insignificant little pebble. But I was so scared that it seemed better than nothing.

So I spoke to it.

"Hello… my pumpkin! Well, yes… I'm afraid. Silly, isn't it? But that's how it is… I'm afraid they'll mock me… that they won't understand me… I'm afraid they'll sack me…"

It was the strangest thing. I felt I was *becoming* Miss Charlotte. I was tall and strong.

I put Gertrude back under my hat and walked calmly to the centre of the stage. There I strolled up and down a bit, smiling gently. Then I sat down behind Miss Charlotte's desk and delicately took off my hat – like a witch's hat but with a round top instead of a long, pointy one – and took my precious little pebble off my head. I caressed it a little. And I talked and talked and talked…

I poured my heart out to my pebble. I spoke loudly so that all three hundred people in the audience could hear me.

They had to understand. They had to realize what kind of teacher I was.

Afterwards I gently placed Gertrude on my desk. The second act was about to start. To prove to everyone that Miss Charlotte was a good teacher, I tested their spelling and maths.

My pupils were amazing. Thomas's mother shouted: "Well done!" when her son correctly spelt "oesophagus" with "oe" and "ph". And Aurore, who could barely do simple additions before Miss Charlotte's arrival, managed to do four complicated multiplications in a row.

Three pupils presented their projects. But this time, no one threw a spanner in the works, as neither Mr Cracpote, nor the other teachers, nor the parents interrupted the presentations. Everything was explained to them properly. When Benoît did his thing again with the shepherd's pie, a fair few parents laughed heartily.

To finish it off, I decided to improvise. We hadn't planned a third act, but never mind! So, just like that, in front of everyone and without thinking or worrying about what they'd say or how they'd react, I invented a story. I don't even know where it came from. Nor where it went... Once I'd finished my tale, I barely remembered any of it.

I was crawling on all fours through a narrow passage in a cave... When I shone my pocket light along the walls I could see millions of tiny and yet extraordinarily bright stones. I felt neither hunger nor cold.

That's all I remember.

Oh, wait, no... There were... yes... yes... there were people. Men and women, and children too, no doubt. As tiny as mice, as baby mice even. No... tinier still. Elves? Goblins?

They were climbing a wall. They were connected by teeny-weeny cords.

I was fascinated.

Suddenly the earth trembled as if a sleeping giant were slowly waking up from a deep slumber. Were we in a cave, somewhere in another dimension, or simply in the belly of an ogre?

That's when the wall began to crack and…

But none of that matters. What matters is that when Charles-Antoine drew the curtains, a heavy silence came over the audience. There wasn't a single sound for about ten seconds. My heart was racing like mad.

Suddenly there was a ripple of applause. Phew! We'd done it! I was almost certain of it.

Mr Cracpote addressed the audience. And to be honest, I was rather impressed with him. Our head teacher said they shouldn't take any rash decisions. He was going to meet with Miss Charlotte to clear up the business of her qualifications and, without forbidding her to teach "differently", he'd recommend her not to "go too far". That sounded like a good compromise to me.

"I am hopeful that we'll find common ground," he finally declared in his thick, serious voice.

This time round the applause came from behind the curtain. And a thunderous applause it was!

But Miss Charlotte's story doesn't end here.

Chapter 8

Lots of Kisses and a Fleeting Image

I should have been happy. All my friends congratulated me while we moved the desks back to the classroom next door.

Charles-Antoine walked me home, and we talked about new projects we could do, but my heart wasn't in it.

Later, when I was lying in bed, I couldn't sleep. There was one thing... a memory, an image... that haunted me.

Suddenly I cried out: "Aaaargh!"

For a brief moment I saw it again.

It had happened when I was telling my story, while I was playing the part of Miss Charlotte on stage. I was describing the cave with the sparkling walls when she appeared in the window, the middle one, high up on the side of the assembly hall.

I saw Miss Charlotte. She looked at me and smiled.

And then she disappeared.

I slipped on some clothes over my pyjamas and ran to the door. Outside the air was mild.

I nearly got lost. It was not a neighbourhood I'd been to very often. Certainly not at night! But it wasn't long before I recognized Miss Charlotte's street…

Charles-Antoine was there, outside the house, next to the garden gnomes. He'd guessed it too.

Our new teacher was gone.

She'd left during the meeting in the assembly hall.

I sat down next to Charles-Antoine. I gently put my head on his shoulder. There are moments when it's very important to have friends.

Charles-Antoine held a sheet of paper in his hands. I slowly read what Miss Charlotte had written.

Dear friends,
I spent a couple a fabulous weeks with you.
I thank you…
   I would have liked to stay a little longer, but another school very far from here requires my services. Their Year 5 teacher has caught the whooping cough…

I know that you can manage on your own now. Each of you has tons of plans in his or her head, and you have millions of stories teeming in your brains. Talk about them to your next teacher. Don't be afraid. I am sure that he (or she) will understand.

I will often think of you all, and I hope that every time you have a chat with your toothbrush or shoelaces you will think of me a little too.

A million kisses,

Miss Charlotte

PS: This afternoon I saw a young girl who looked a lot like me on stage in the assembly hall. I want her to have Gertrude. My poor pumpkin is tired of travelling... One day, perhaps, I'll come back for her.

Charles-Antoine lifted up one of the garden gnomes, and there was Gertrude.

She looked very small and lonely. I took her in my hands and stroked her a bit.

Epilogue

Gertrude has been living with me for two months now. I talk to her a lot, every day. And every time I think of Miss Charlotte.

Sometimes I think I recognize our teacher in the street when I see an old, tall and skinny lady. I imagine her wearing a hat, like a witch's hat but with a round top instead of a long, pointy one.

But each time I'm disappointed. It's never Miss Charlotte.

At school a new teacher has taken her place. His name is Henri and he is very friendly. He even accepted that we work very hard in the morning in order to do things that are a bit wackier in the afternoon. But still, we miss Miss Charlotte.

A lot.

Soon school will be over. I can't wait for the holidays to start. Henri is not coming back in September. Nor is our old teacher. She decided to spend a whole year looking after her baby.

I'm wondering what our new teacher will look like. It would be amazing if Miss Charlotte were to return!

Sometimes, when I talk to Gertrude at night, I have the feeling that Miss Charlotte can hear me. Then I tell myself that maybe my original suspicion was correct: what if Miss Charlotte really did come from another planet? Maybe she's travelling through space right now, billions of light years away. And yet she sees and hears everything thanks to her pebble.

I know that this may seem a little crazy. But can you really be sure?

THE END